BRAIN GAMES

GAMES

for

clever

Kids

Puzzles and solutions created
by Dr Gareth Moore
B.Sc (Hons) M.Phil Ph.D

Illustrations by Chris Dickason

Edited by Sophie Schrey

Cover design by Angie Allison

BRAIN GAMES

for clever Kids

Buster Books

First published in Great Britain in 2014 by Buster Books,
an imprint of Michael O'Mara Books Limited,
9 Lion Yard, Tremadoc Road, London SW4 7NQ

 www.mombooks.com/buster

Buster Books

@BusterBooks

Puzzles and solutions © Gareth Moore

Illustrations and layouts © Buster Books 2014

A CIP catalogue record for this book is available from the British Library.

ISBN: 978-1-78055-249-1

18 20 19 17

Papers used by Buster Books are natural, recyclable products
made from wood grown in sustainable forests. The manufacturing processes
conform to the environmental regulations of the country of origin.

Printed and bound in February 2019 by CPI Group (UK) Ltd,
108 Beddington Lane, Croydon, CR0 4YY, United Kingdom

MIX
Paper from
responsible sources
FSC® C020471

INTRODUCTION

Are you ready for a challenge? This book contains
101 Brain Game puzzles which are designed to test every
part of your brain. Each Brain Game can be tackled on
its own, but the puzzles get steadily harder as the book
progresses so you might want to start at the front and
work your way through.

At the top of every page, there is a space for you to write
how much time it took you to complete each game. Don't
be afraid to make notes on the pages – this can be a good
tactic to help you keep track of your thoughts as you work
on a puzzle. There are some blank pages at the back of the
book which you can use for working out your answers.

Read the simple instructions on each page before tackling
a puzzle. If you get stuck, read the instructions again in
case there's something you missed. Work in pencil so you
can rub things out and have another try.

INTRODUCTION

You could also try asking an adult, although did you know that your brain is actually much more powerful than a grown-up's? When you get older, your brain will get rid of lots of bits it thinks it doesn't need any more, which means you might be better at solving these games than older people are.

If you're really stuck have a peek at the answers at the back of the book, and then try and work out how you could have got to that solution yourself.

Now, good luck and have fun!

Introducing the Brain Games Master, Dr Gareth Moore

Dr Gareth Moore is an Ace Puzzler, and author of lots of puzzle and brain-training books.

He created an online brain-training site called BrainedUp.com, and runs an online puzzle site called PuzzleMix.com. Gareth has a PhD from the University of Cambridge, where he taught machines to understand spoken English.

Can you draw lines to connect each pair of identical
shapes together? The lines must not cross or touch each
other, and only one line is allowed in each grid square.
You can't use diagonal lines.

This example solution
shows how it works:

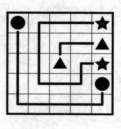

a.

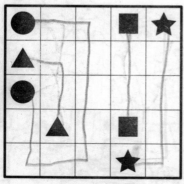

b.

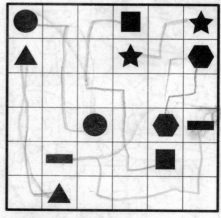

Use your brainpower to climb these word ladders. Each ladder has one word at the top and another at the bottom. All you have to do is fill in the empty steps between the bottom word and the top word.

At each step change just one letter to make a new word.

For example, you could link **APE** to **OWL** like this:

APE ➝ AWE ➝ OWE ➝ OWL

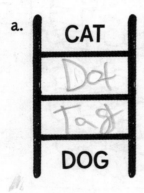

a.

CAT

Dot

Tag

DOG

b.

MUM*e*

mad

mad

DAD

c.

THE

Tin

Hen

WIN

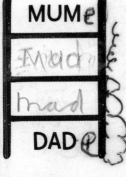

BRAIN GAME 3

 Time ....

The three pieces needed to finish this jigsaw have been mixed up with some from a different puzzle. Can you work out which of the loose pieces you need to complete this picture?

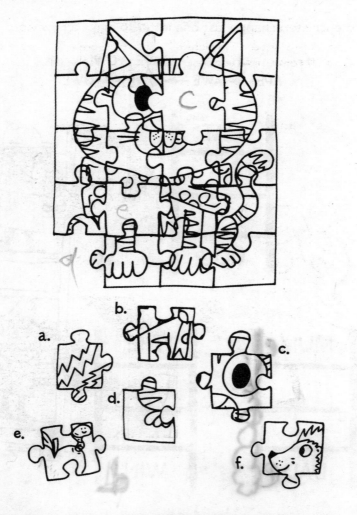

Can you count how many building block cubes there are in each of these 3D pictures? Make sure you don't forget to count any cubes hidden behind or beneath the cubes you can see.

For example in this picture there are 4 cubes:

a.

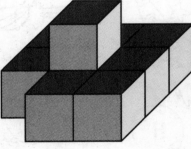

b.

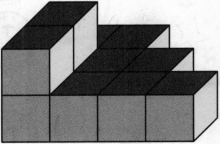

BRAIN GAME 5

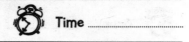 Time ....

How many three-letter words can you find by travelling inwards from the outside ring of planets to the centre ring, picking one letter from each ring in turn? For example, you could pick 'H', 'I' and 'T' to spell 'HIT'. 3, 2, 1 ... blast off!

EASY TARGET: 5 words
MEDIUM TARGET: 10 words
HARD TARGET: 15 words

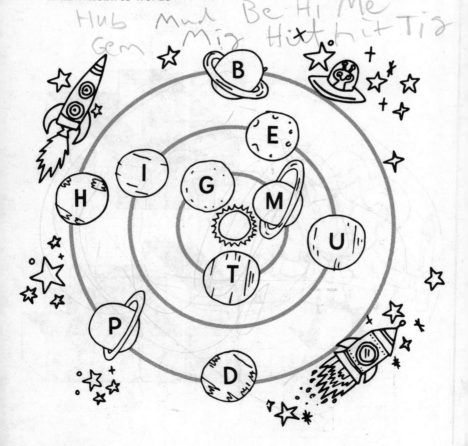

Use your powers of logic to work out which grid squares contain hidden mines.

The Rules

- There can be a mine in any empty grid square, but not in any of the numbered squares.

- A number in a square tells you how many mines there are in touching squares, including diagonally.

Have a look at this example solution to see how it works:

		1
☼	3	☼
1	3	☼

Now try these three puzzles:

a.

1	1	2	1
		2	
2	3		2
	2		

b.

1			
2	3	3	
		2		1
		O	

c.

	1	1	O	
			2	1
1	3		4	
	2		5	
		2		

BRAIN GAME 7

Just like a secret spy, can you crack these mirror-based codes?

Code 1

Certain capital letters, such as A and H, are symmetrical. This means they look exactly the same when you write them on a piece of paper, fold them in half vertically and then hold them against a mirror, like this:

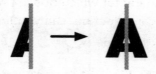

If you cross out all of the letters which are vertically symmetrical, can you work out the coded message hidden in the strange sentence below?

BAIT EVEN MOTHS WITH THE HEN!

Code 2

Some capital letters are also symmetrical when reflected horizontally in a mirror, like this:

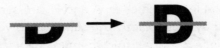

Another coded message has been received. By crossing out any letter or character which doesn't have either horizontal or vertical reflection, can you find another hidden message?

MAN DECOY DEN BY LOGS OK?

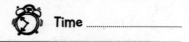
In Star Land there are four different types of coin, each with a different value. There is a 1 star coin, a 2 star coin, a 5 star coin and a 10 star coin. They look like this:

a. What is the minimum number of star coins you need to spend exactly 48 stars?

b. What is the minimum number of star coins you need to buy something that costs 27 stars?

c. You wish to buy an item, but you're not sure if it costs 22 stars or 33 stars. What is the minimum number of coins you need to have with you so that you can make up either exactly 22 or exactly 33 stars?

d. If you had a 100-star banknote, and you bought something which cost 63 stars, what is the minimum number of coins you can receive in your change?

Are you daredevil enough to take on the domino puzzle challenge? You must place the five loose dominoes on to the shaded dominoes in order to build a complete domino loop. Dominoes can only touch each other if they have the same number of spots on the touching ends.

BRAIN GAME 10

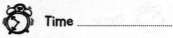 Time ....

Can you find the 10 differences between these two very similar pictures?

Complete this sudoku puzzle by placing a number from 1 to 6 in every square, but with no number appearing more than once in each row, column or marked three-by-two area.

BRAIN GAME 12

Help the workers locate their equipment. Using only two straight lines, divide the factory into three areas, with each area containing one worker, one paintbrush and one helmet. The lines you draw must start at one edge of the factory and cross all the way to another edge of the factory.

TOP TIP: Use a ruler or the edge of another book to check that your lines are straight!

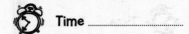

Can you find all of the items from a toy sale in the wordsearch grid below? They might be written forwards, backwards, up, down or diagonally.

C	I	T	E	L	T	K	P	A	I	N	T	S	E	T
A	A	O	T	L	B	N	D	S	N	P	M	T	S	E
C	Y	P	A	E	R	O	P	L	A	N	E	A	L	S
T	O	G	O	I	S	D	A	M	I	K	P	Z	O	N
I	E	H	E	T	T	L	Y	R	C	D	Z	P	T	O
O	C	S	E	E	G	E	E	A	D	U	R	R	S	I
N	L	S	Y	L	P	N	R	D	P	G	A	I	I	T
F	R	S	I	R	I	R	I	W	O	C	A	C	P	C
I	U	O	N	D	T	C	A	N	G	M	D	M	R	U
G	W	F	O	T	G	S	O	N	N	N	A	I	E	R
U	E	P	O	R	G	N	I	P	P	I	K	S	T	T
R	E	Z	A	I	O	C	I	M	T	C	P	R	A	S
E	N	G	J	N	A	E	Z	Y	E	E	K	S	W	N
D	N	E	K	R	W	C	Y	N	L	H	R	G	Y	O
D	R	A	O	B	Y	E	K	G	S	F	C	A	G	C

ACTION FIGURE   HELICOPTER   RACKET

AEROPLANE   JIGSAW PUZZLE   SKIPPING ROPE

BOARD GAME   KEYBOARD   SPINNING TOP

CHEMISTRY SET   MODEL SET   WATER PISTOL

CONSTRUCTION SET   PAINT SET

FLYING DISC   RACING CAR

Look at these creepy-crawly bugs ...

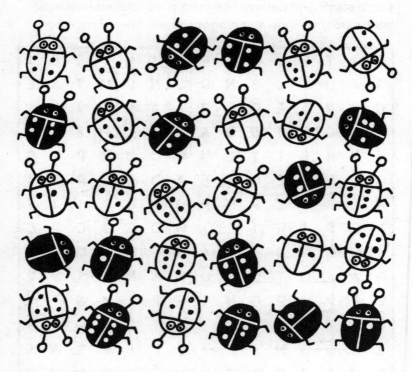

a. How many bugs are there in total?

b. Are there more white bugs or more black bugs?

c. How many bugs have the same number of spots as legs?

d. How many bugs have an odd number of spots?

e. How many bugs have antennae and more than three spots?

Can you draw straight lines to join all of the dots into a single loop? You can only use straight horizontal or vertical lines, and the loop can't cross or touch itself. Parts of the line have already been drawn in to get you started.

Here's an example solution. Notice how it uses every dot:

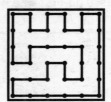

a.

b.

BRAIN GAME 16

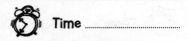

Time ....

Can you solve this crossword where all of the clues are written inside the grid? The arrows show which grid squares their solutions go in, and all the words are written left to right or top to bottom no matter which way the arrow points. The first one has been done for you.

A period of 100 years ▼		Taxi ►			
M	**E**	**L**	**O**	**D**	**Y**
A tune		There are five of these on each foot ►			
►			Baby's bed		Short 'goodbye' ▲
			Allow		A dividing space ▼
Past tense of eat		What your foot attaches to ►	▼		
►				Really love ▲	
Tall, long-lived plant		Where water comes out ►			

Can your brain handle the 'Super Jigsaw Sudoku'? Solve the puzzle by placing a number from 1 to 6 in every square, but with no number appearing more than once in each row, column or bold-lined jigsaw-shaped area.

1	3				
6		2	3	1	
					4
2					
	5	1	2		3
				4	2

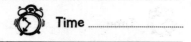
By drawing along the existing lines, can you divide this shape up into four identical pieces, with no unused parts left over? If you imagine cutting the shape up into these four pieces, then each piece would have to be exactly the same once you rotated them all to point the same way. You can't turn any pieces over.

Have a look at this example. Can you see how you would have four identical shapes if you cut them out along the thick lines and made them all point the same way?

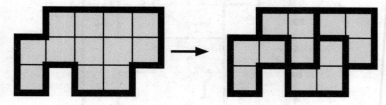

TOP TIP: Start by working out how big each piece must be. Because all the pieces must be the same size, you can count the number of grid squares and divide by 4 to calculate this.

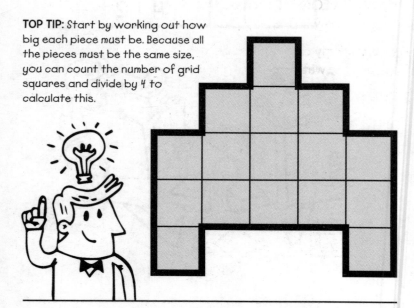

An anagram is a word that can be made by rearranging the letters of another word. For example, LEMON is an anagram of MELON.

Unscramble the anagrams below to fill in the missing words in these sentences. Each missing word is an anagram of the word written in capital letters in the same sentence.

a. It's funny how a CAT will sometimes _ _ _ the fool.

b. My cat used its PAWS to swat a flying _ _ _ _ .

c. A cat won't _ _ _ _ _ far from its food TRAYS.

d. When it hears thunder _ _ _ _ _ , my cat grabs hold of me with a tight CLASP.

e. My cat LOOPED the loop when it saw a _ _ _ _ _ _ walk past the window.

f. I think my cat wants to be a _ _ _ _ _ _ . I CRANED my neck to watch it moving to music.

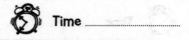

What number comes next in each of these mathematical sequences?

a. 1   3   5   7   ___

b. 2   4   8   16   _3_

c. 2   5   8   11   ___

d. 81   27   9   3   ___

e. 4   5   7   10   ___

Solve these Futoshiki puzzles by placing the numbers 1 to 3 **(Puzzle a)** or 1 to 4 **(Puzzle b)** once each into every row and column.

You must obey the 'greater than' signs. These are arrows which always point from the bigger number to the smaller number of a pair. For example, you could have '2 > 1' since 2 is greater than 1, but '1 > 2' would be wrong because 1 is not greater in value than 2.

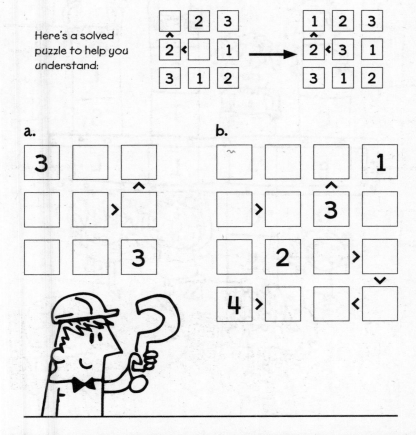

BRAIN GAME 22

 Time ....

Imagine sliding these columns of letters up and down to make different words through the horizontal window. One letter should remain visible through the window in each column. How many words, each of four letters, can you make? One word is made already.

EASY TARGET: 5 words
MEDIUM TARGET: 10 words
HARD TARGET: 15 words

Complete this sudoku puzzle by placing a number from 1 to 6 in every square, but with no number appearing more than once in each row, column or marked three-by-two area.

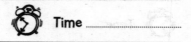

Using just your imagination, see if you can work out what number you would be able to form if you were to cut out and rearrange the positions of these six tiles. There's no need to rotate any of the pieces – just imagine sliding them to new positions.

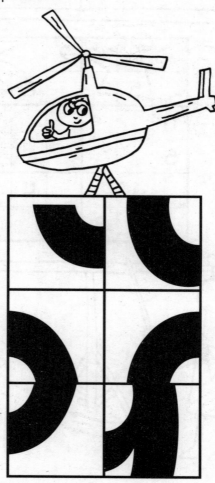

Find out what's cooking in the cauldron by rearranging these letters in order to spell out three racket sports. All of the letters should be used once each.

BRAIN GAME 26

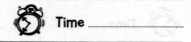

Tickle your brain with this crisscross puzzle. Your mission is to fit all of the listed words into the grid, crossword-style.

TOP TIP: You could start by adding the nine-letter word in.

3 letters
End
Fed
Nap
Sum

4 letters
Byte
Chef
Dust
Even
Flea
Here

Loud
Mute
Name
Open
Taut
Tuba

5 letters
Attic
Label

9 letters
Chocolate

To solve these Calcudoku puzzles, place 1 to 3 once each into every row and column. You must place these numbers so that each bold-lined set of grid squares equals the small clue number printed in it when you write the clue's mathematical sign between the numbers in that area.

Look at this example:

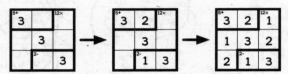

- The top-left bold-lined area contains a 3 and a 2. The small clue in that area has a '5' and a '+'. 3 + 2 = 5, so the empty box in this area must contain a 2.

- Now look at the '2-' area. You need to find a number that can be subtracted to result in 2. You know that 3 - 1 = 2, so the missing number must be a 1. For minus areas, always start with the bigger number and subtract the smaller one.

- Now you can solve the big '12x' area. You can't repeat a number in a row or column, so the top-right square must be a 1 and the bottom-left square must be a 2. The rest of the area can be filled in the same way. 1 x 1 x 3 x 2 x 2 = 12, so you know you're correct.

a.

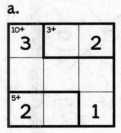

b.

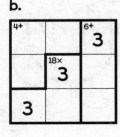

c.

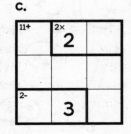

Can you match each monster with its identical twin?

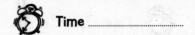

Can you use this word circle to solve the following clues? Make words that use the central letter plus two or more of the other letters, for example, RAN. You can start with any letter, but you can't use a letter more than once in a word.

The Clues

a. One of the colours on a traffic light.

b. The first word you might write in a letter, to address it to somebody.

c. This is all around you, and we breathe it.

d. Water goes down this when you run the tap.

e. What you are doing right now as you look at these words!

f. A telephone will do this when someone is calling.

g. This is water that falls from the sky.

h. A grassy area attached to a house.

i. If you're very brave, you are this.

j. A single piece of sand is called this.

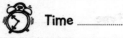 Time ....

Can you solve these brain chains in your head, without writing anything down?

Start with the value at the top of each column (which is always 7 in these three puzzles), then follow each arrow in turn and do what the maths instructions say until you reach the empty box. Write your final answer in that box.

For example in the first column you would start with 7, then subtract 5, then add 3 to the result you have so far, and so on until the bottom.

a.

7
−5
+3
×2
−4
÷2

b.

7
+2
÷3
×2
−1
+3

c.

7
×6
+5
−6
+11
÷4

Can you find the words hidden in this grid of letters to solve the clues below? Start on any letter and then keep moving to any letter in a touching box, including ones that touch diagonally, to spell out a word. You can't use a letter more than once in any word.

For example, you could start on 'L', move to 'A' and then to 'G' to spell 'LAG'.

U	A	H	E
L	G	T	R

The Clues

a. If you've already eaten something, you say that you
_ _ _ it. (3 letters)

b. This is another word for a witch, or an ugly old woman.
_ _ _ (3 letters)

c. If you're not on time for school, then you are _ _ _ _.
(4 letters)

d. If you choose to put something off, you say that you
will do it _ _ _ _ _. (5 letters)

e. If you use a lot of soap and water, you build
up a _ _ _ _ _ _. (6 letters)

Extra challenge!
Can you find a word that uses every single letter?

BRAIN GAME 32

Complete these puzzles by drawing lines to represent bridges between the numbered 'islands'.

The Rules

- You can only draw horizontal or vertical bridges, and each island must have the same number of bridges leading off it as the number printed inside the island.

- Bridges can't cross each other, or fly above an island.

- One line represents one bridge. There can be no more than two bridges directly joining any pair of islands.

- You must arrange the set of bridges so that someone could walk from one island to any other island, just using the bridges you've drawn.

Here's an example to help you understand:

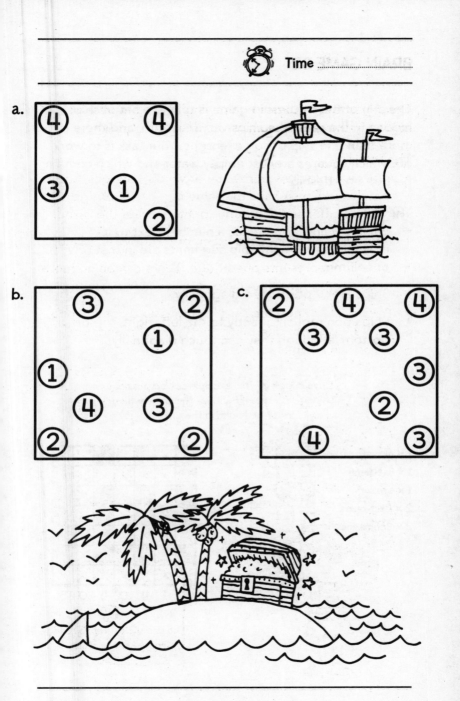

BRAIN GAME 33

The aim of this battleship game is to find a set of ships hidden in the grid. The ships vary in length, and there is more than one ship of some lengths. Your task is to work out which squares are just empty water and which contain part of a battleship.

The Rules
- Each row and column has a number next to it indicating how many ship segments are in that row or column.

- Ships aren't positioned diagonally.

- Ships don't touch directly to the left, right, top or bottom (although they can touch diagonally).

Have a look at this example solved puzzle. The grid on the left shows the ships which must be found in the grid:

1 × Aircraft carrier

1 × Battleship

1 × Cruiser

2 × Destroyers

3 × Submarines

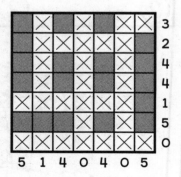

The crosses in this puzzle represent water.

TOP TIPS:

- You could start by putting a small cross in the squares which you know must be water because the rows or columns are marked with a '0'.

- When you have filled in the squares that you definitely know are a whole ship, don't forget to mark all of the squares alongside it as water.

Now try and find the following battleships in the grid below.

1 × Aircraft carrier
1 × Battleship
1 × Cruiser
2 × Destroyers
3 × Submarines

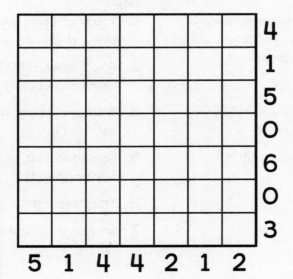

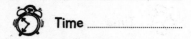
Can you solve the clues to complete this crossword puzzle?

Across

1. Sometimes made of wax, you might use this to colour in (6)

4. Gift (7)

6. Rose and tulips are these (7)

8. Small laugh (6)

Down

1. You might sing one of these at Christmas (5)

2. Another word for TV commercials (3)

3. A squirrel might like to eat this (3)

5. Someone who cares for sick people (5)

6. Thick mist (3)

7. Movement of a dog's tail (3)

Complete this sudoku puzzle by placing a number from
1 to 8 in every square, but with no number appearing more
than once in each row, column or marked four-by-two area.

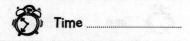
Can you crack these real-life sequence codes? Each sequence is made up of a connected set of words in a particular order, but you're only shown the first letter of each word. Using the given clues, can you work out what the hidden words should be?

Have a look at this example:

M   T   W   T   F   S   S

CLUE: You'd find these on a calendar.

ANSWER: Monday, Tuesday, Wednesday, Thursday, Friday, Saturday, Sunday (days of the week in order)

a. JFMAMJJASOND

b. ROYGBIV

c. OTTFFSSENT

d. FSTFFSSENT

CLUE A: You would find all of these in order in a diary.

CLUE B: What can you sometimes see when the sun starts shining after rain? You can also see these reflected off the shiny part of a DVD, or when you blow a bubble.

CLUE C: Try counting aloud.

CLUE D: There's something in common between this sequence and the previous one. Try thinking about the results of a race.

Use your brainpower to complete this linesweeper puzzle. The aim is to draw a single loop in the grid made up of just straight lines.

The Rules

- No diagonal lines are allowed.

- The loop can't cross or touch itself, and can only pass through empty grid squares.

- The squares with numbers in tell you how many touching squares the loop passes through including diagonally-touching squares.

Have a look at this example. Can you see how the square with the number '8' in has all 8 touching squares used by the loop around it?

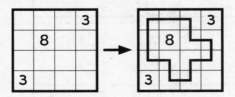

a.

3				
		4	5	
		5		

b.

				3
			8	
			6	
				2

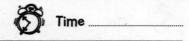
Get your brain in gear for the 'Greater-Than Sudoku' challenge. The same rules apply as for a normal sudoku but there's a twist.

- You must place the numbers 1 to 6 once each into every row, column and marked three-by-two area.

- The twist is that there are also 'greater than' signs (>) which you must follow. These are arrows which always point at the smaller number of a pair. For example, 2 > 1 because 2 is greater in value than 1.

Can you find the baby animals hidden in this wordsearch grid? They can be written in any direction, including diagonally, and either forwards or backwards.

```
F  K  I  T  T  E  N  D  P  O  P  G  L  J  Y
I  F  V  O  L  C  H  I  C  K  N  G  K  G  P
G  E  F  O  A  L  A  P  N  I  N  N  U  Y
K  F  N  E  F  F  G  A  L  I  O  I  U  I  H
L  E  E  L  A  G  T  S  L  L  L  L  E  L
I  I  N  W  V  L  O  Y  N  G  L  K  G  C  E
D  R  N  G  G  G  G  N  A  T  C  L  C  V
L  I  G  Y  K  N  N  G  M  E  A  U  N  A  E
K  C  K  N  F  T  O  B  L  E  O  D  C  U  R
D  C  F  R  Y  Y  I  G  U  J  Y  G  P  L  E
T  C  P  F  G  P  I  G  O  G  L  C  P  S  T
M  A  U  L  K  P  H  E  C  L  K  J  F  C  E
E  L  P  Y  W  M  Y  O  I  G  A  E  N  L  G
N  F  P  M  L  Y  U  C  K  E  O  S  B  U  C
E  O  Y  L  Y  O  E  U  T  C  V  N  O  T  C
```

CALF	FOAL	KITTEN
CHICK	FRY	LAMB
CUB	GOSLING	LEVERET
DUCKLING	JOEY	PIGLET
FAWN	KID	PUPPY

BRAIN GAME 40

Can you draw lines to connect each pair of identical shapes together? The lines must not cross or touch each other, and only one line is allowed in each grid square. You can't use diagonal lines.

This example solution shows how it works:

There's a vowel thief on the loose! Can you stop him by putting the vowels back to reveal what the original words were?

For example: XMPL ➡ **EXAMPLE**

a. PLNTY

b. MRK

c. DRMNG

d. KTCHN

e. RPLN

f. BNN

g. TLVSN

h. RDVRK

Look at all of these flowers.

a. How many flowers have at least three solid black petals?

b. How many leaves can you count in total?

c. How many flowers have a black centre and more than two leaves?

d. Are there more black or more white petals in total?

e. How many flowers have more leaves than petals?

How quickly can you crack these codes to find hidden words? To solve them you must delete one letter from each pair.

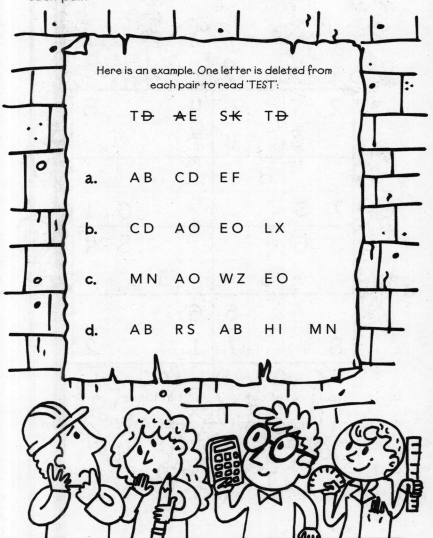

Here is an example. One letter is deleted from each pair to read 'TEST':

T~~D~~ ~~A~~E S~~K~~ T~~D~~

a.   A B   C D   E F

b.   C D   A O   E O   L X

c.   M N   A O   W Z   E O

d.   A B   R S   A B   H I   M N

BRAIN GAME 44

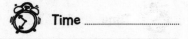

Complete this sudoku puzzle by placing a number from
1 to 8 in every square, but with no number appearing more
than once in each row, column or marked four-by-two area.

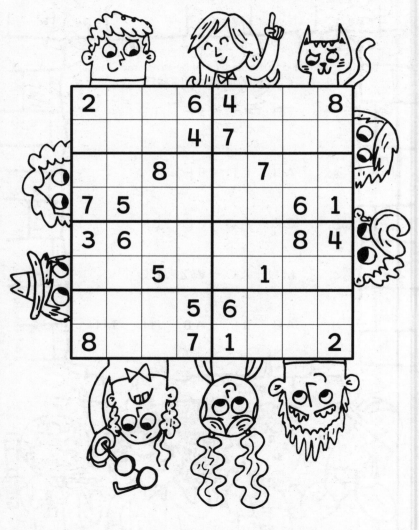

Find find five identical pairs of crazy plants.

BRAIN GAME 46

 Time ....

Can you draw straight lines to join all of the dots into a single loop? You can only use straight horizontal or vertical lines, and the loop can't cross or touch itself. Parts of the line have already been drawn in to get you started.

Here's an example solution. Notice how it uses every dot:

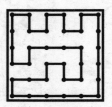

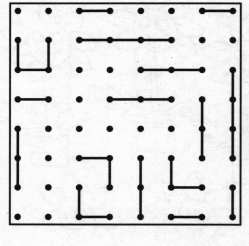

Get ready for the cube challenge! Can you count how many building block cubes there are in this 3D picture?

Look at this example. If you start with a 2-wide by 2-tall by 2-deep construction and take away one of the front cubes, you are left with 7 cubes:

Now try to solve this puzzle. The construction was a 5 wide by 4 tall by 3 deep cuboid but some of the cubes have been taken from from the front side, which you can see. How many cubes are left?

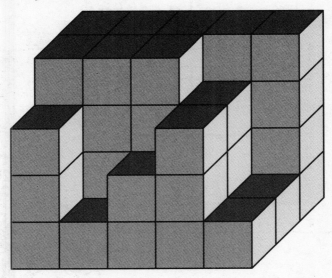

TOP TIP: Try counting each layer of cubes separately. For example, how many cubes are there on the bottom layer, where nothing has been removed? You can calculate this by multiplying the depth (3 cubes) by the width (5 cubes), since you can see there are 3 rows each of 5 cubes on that layer.

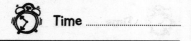
Get your brain in gear for the 'Greater-Than Sudoku'
challenge. The same rules apply as for a normal sudoku.

The Rules

- You must place the numbers 1 to 6 once each into
  every row, column and marked three-by-two area.

- The twist is that there are also 'greater than' signs
  which you must follow. These are arrows which always
  point at the smaller number of a pair. For example,
  2 > 1 because 2 is greater in value than 1.

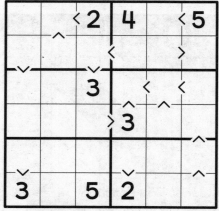

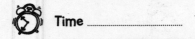

This grid of letters contains the words to solve the clues below. To play, start on any letter and then keep moving to any touching letter, including diagonally-touching letters, to spell out a word. You can't use a letter square more than once in any word (but if the letters are on different grid squares that's okay). For example, you could start on 'M', move to 'O', to 'S' and then finally the other 'S' to spell 'MOSS'.

P	M	S	S
R	O	I	E

The Clues

a. A short word for the 'opposite' of a brother.
_ _ _ (3 letters)

b. This is something you might do for a photograph.
_ _ _ _ (4 letters)

c. When you're older and finish school, this is the name of a big dance often held in your final year.
_ _ _ _ (4 letters)

d. You can use this to clean the floor. _ _ _ (3 letters)

e. This is a type of flower, often thought to be romantic.
_ _ _ _ (4 letters)

Extra Challenge

Can you find a word that uses every single letter?

BRAIN GAME 50

The aim of this battleship game is to find a set of ships hidden in the grid. The ships vary in length, and there is more than one ship of some lengths. Your task is to work out which squares are just empty water and which contain part of a battleship.

The Rules

- Each row and column has a number next to it indicating how many ship segments are in that row or column.

- Ships aren't positioned diagonally.

- Ships don't touch directly to the left, right, top or bottom (although they can touch diagonally).

Have a look at this example solved puzzle. The grid on the left shows the ships which must be found in the grid.

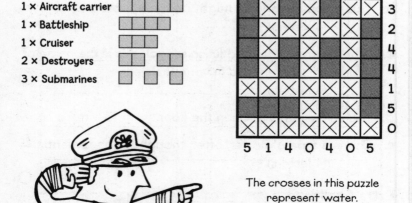

1 × Aircraft carrier
1 × Battleship
1 × Cruiser
2 × Destroyers
3 × Submarines

The crosses in this puzzle represent water.

TOP TIPS:

- Try starting by putting a small cross in the squares which you know must be water because the rows or columns are marked with a '0'.

- When you have filled in the squares that you definitely know are a whole ship, don't forget to mark all of the squares alongside it as water.

Now try and find the following battleships in the grid below.

1 × Aircraft carrier
1 × Battleship
2 × Cruisers
2 × Destroyers
3 × Submarines

Row clues (top to bottom): 1 2 7 2 0 4 0 2 4 0

Column clues (left to right): 1 1 4 2 3 0 7 0 1 3

BRAIN GAME 51

Use your brain strength to climb these word ladders. Each ladder has one word at the top and another at the bottom, and all you have to do is fill in the empty steps between the bottom word and the top word.

At each step change just one letter to make a new word. Don't rearrange any of the letters.

For example, you could link **LOVE** to **MILK** like this:

LOVE ➡ **MOVE** ➡ **MOLE** ➡ **MILE** ➡ **MILK**

a. **HARD**

TIME

b. **LONG**

GAME

Time ....

Can you find the 10 differences between these two very similar pictures?

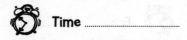

Are you daredevil enough to take on the domino puzzle challenge? You must place the ten loose dominoes on to the shaded dominoes in order to build a complete domino loop. Dominoes can only touch each other if they have the same number of spots on the touching ends.

Using only two straight lines, divide the submarine window into four areas, with each area containing one diver, one shark and one jellyfish. The lines must cross from one edge of the circle all the way to another edge. The lines will need to cross each other in order to divide the window into four areas.

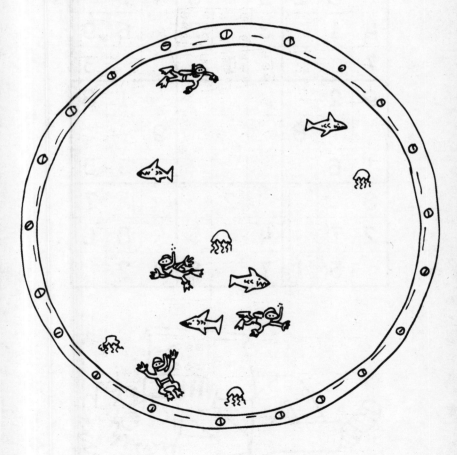

BRAIN GAME 55

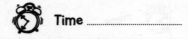 Time ....

Sudoku time! Can you solve the puzzle by placing the numbers 1 to 9 once each into every row, column and marked three-by-three area?

	8	2	9			6	4	7	
4	1		3			2		6	9
7				1					3
9	2							1	8
		8				9			
1	6							3	5
8				2					7
2	7		4		5			8	6
	5	1	7		8	3	2		

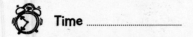
Can you solve these brain chains in your head, without writing anything down?

Start with the value at the top of each column, then follow each arrow in turn and do what the maths instructions say until you reach the empty box. You can then write your final answer in that box.

For example in the first column you would start with 16, then divide by 4, then multiply the result you have so far by 6, and so on until you reach the bottom of the chain.

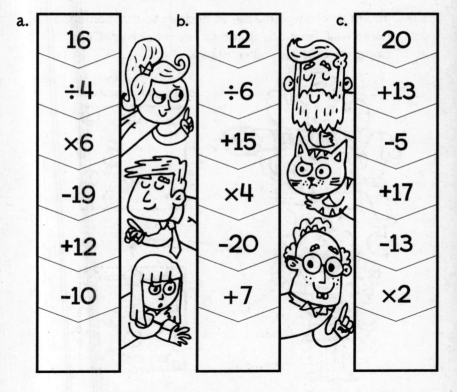

a.
16
÷4
×6
-19
+12
-10

b.
12
÷6
+15
×4
-20
+7

c.
20
+13
-5
+17
-13
×2

BRAIN GAME 57

Complete this puzzle by drawing lines to represent bridges between the numbered 'islands'.

The Rules

- You can only draw horizontal or vertical bridges, and each island must have the same number of bridges leading off it as the number printed inside the island.

- Bridges can't cross each other, or fly above an island.

- One line represents one bridge. There can be no more than two bridges directly joining any pair of islands.

- You must arrange the set of bridges so that someone could walk from one island to any other island, just using the bridges you've drawn.

Here's an example to help you understand:

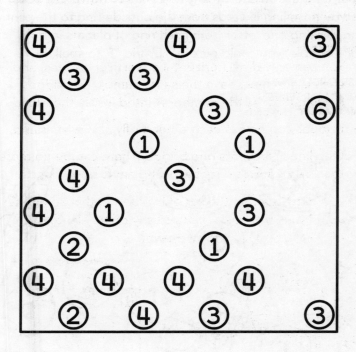

BRAIN GAME 58

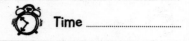

Time for blast off! How many three-letter words can you find by travelling inwards from the outside ring to the centre ring, picking one letter from each ring of planets in turn? For example, you could pick 'B', 'E' and 'T' to spell 'BET'.

EASY TARGET: 5 words
MEDIUM TARGET: 10 words
HARD TARGET: 15 words

Boggle your brain with 'windoku', a special kind of sudoku puzzle. Your challenge is to place the numbers 1 to 9 once each into every row, column, marked three-by-three area, as well as each of the four shaded three-by-three areas.

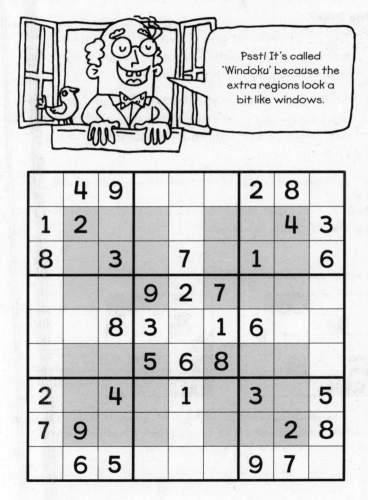

Psst! It's called 'Windoku' because the extra regions look a bit like windows.

BRAIN GAME 60

Is your brain ready to shine? The aim of this game is to place lamps into the correct empty grid squares so that every remaining empty square is lit up by at least one lamp.

The Rules

- Lamps shine along grid squares in the same row or column right up to the first black square they come across. They don't shine diagonally.

- Some of the shaded squares contain numbers. These tell you exactly how many of the touching squares (up, down, left or right, but not diagonally) must contain lamps.

- A lamp isn't allowed to shine on any other lamp.

- You can place lamps on any empty square so long as the rules are followed.

Look at this before and after example:

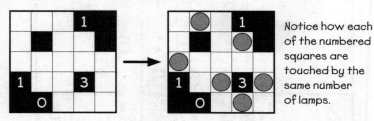

Notice how each of the numbered squares are touched by the same number of lamps.

If you imagine how each light shines, you can see that this is the right solution. Every square is lit up, none of the lights shine on any other and the numbered clues have been followed.

TOP TIP: You can draw in the light shining from each lamp with a dashed line to make it clear.

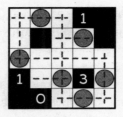

Now see if you can solve these puzzles.

a.

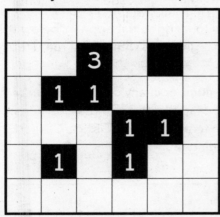

b.

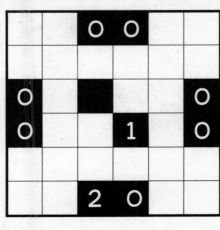

BRAIN GAME 61

Can you conquer these kakuro puzzles by writing a number from 1 to 9 into each of the white squares?

The Rules

- Place the numbers so that each continuous horizontal or vertical run of white squares adds up to the clue number shown in the shaded square to the left or top of that run.

- If a clue number appears above the diagonal line it is the total of the run to its right. If it appears below the diagonal line, then it gives the total of the run directly below the clue.

- You can't repeat a number in any continuous run of white squares. For example, to solve the clue number '4', you would have to use '3' and '1', since '2' and '2' would mean repeating '2'.

Have a look at this before and after example to see how it works:

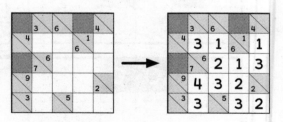

a.

b.

BRAIN GAME 62

Can you place a letter into each of the empty bricks in this word pyramid? When complete, each row will spell out a word that solves its corresponding clue.

Starting from the top and working down, each row contains the same letters as the previous row plus one extra, although they can be in any order.

For example, if the first row contained 'ACE' then the second row might add an 'R' to spell out 'CARE', and the row below that might add a 'T' for 'TRACE'.

a.
b.
c.

The Clues

a. The opposite of 'bottom'.

b. A place where a ship docks.

c. An activity such as football or tennis.

d. A big picture that you might put up on your bedroom wall.

e. A word that means to object to something, or complain.

f. If you put a piece of clear plastic over a book cover then it _ _ _ _ _ _ _ _ the cover.

g. Someone who is watching an event.

a.

b.

c.

d.

e.

f.

g.

If you were to cut out this shape net, you could fold it up to make a six-sided cube, without any sides missing.

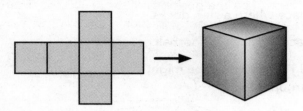

Here are five more shape nets, but only three of them can be used to make a six-sided cube. Which three are these?

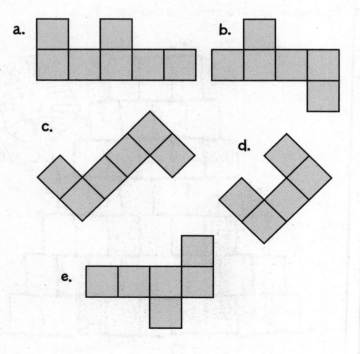

Using just your imagination, see if you can work out what capital letter you would be able to form if you were to cut out and rearrange the positions of these six tiles. There's no need to rotate any of the pieces – just imagine sliding them around.

BRAIN GAME 65

Use your brainpower to complete this linesweeper puzzle. The aim is to draw a single loop in the grid made up of just straight lines.

The Rules

- No diagonal lines are allowed.

- The loop can't cross or touch itself, and can only pass through empty grid squares.

- The squares with numbers in tell you how many touching squares the loop passes through including diagonally-touching squares.

Have a look at this example. Can you see how the square with the number '8' in has all 8 touching squares used by the loop around it?

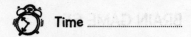

a.

3					3
	5				
		5			
				8	
		5			

b.

					6
		4			
	6				
			7		
3					

BRAIN GAME 66

 Time ....

Can you complete this colourful wordsearch by finding all of the listed words hidden in the grid? They can be written in any direction, including diagonally, either forwards or backwards.

I	W	B	I	T	E	L	O	I	V	G	I	M	L	R
C	N	N	K	E	A	R	G	H	O	A	O	U	W	E
O	T	L	E	C	A	L	I	L	T	R	G	N	H	C
A	C	P	R	N	L	T	D	W	B	O	E	R	O	E
S	V	A	G	R	E	E	N	D	E	M	R	E	T	T
R	H	E	I	G	N	R	I	E	G	L	H	U	P	D
V	I	T	B	G	S	S	I	G	O	G	P	L	A	
I	T	S	E	K	N	I	P	C	I	A	R	W	O	Y
U	Y	E	N	W	O	L	L	E	Y	O	M	T	V	L
K	O	Y	O	U	H	T	G	V	C	A	R	C	N	T
V	U	R	Q	U	T	I	N	A	E	R	N	R	I	C
I	B	R	N	B	O	G	T	R	U	R	I	N	K	U
B	U	E	A	L	U	E	C	E	L	U	C	Y	I	I
T	S	H	R	L	G	L	L	B	B	U	O	L	W	V
G	G	G	E	L	G	B	G	N	I	E	T	H	N	E

BLUE　　　　INDIGO　　　　TURQUOISE
BROWN　　　LILAC　　　　　VIOLET
CREAM　　　MAGENTA　　　WHITE
CYAN　　　　ORANGE　　　　YELLOW
GOLD　　　　PINK
GREEN　　　SILVER

Get your mathematical mind in gear and see if you can work out what number comes next in each of these sequences.

a.   19   16   13   10   ___

b.   2   3   5   7   ___

c.   3   8   13   18   ___

d.   256   64   16   4   ___

e.   4   5   9   14   23   ___

Can you fill in the empty squares so that each grid contains every number from 1 to 16 once each?

The Rules

- You must be able to start at '1' and then move to '2', '3', '4' and so on by moving only to touching grid squares.

- You can only move left, right, up or down between squares, but not diagonally.

This example solution should help make the rules clear:

15	14	9	8
16	13	10	7
1	12	11	6
2	3	4	5

a.

4			7
	10	9	
	11	14	
1			16

b.

12			15
	10	9	
	1	8	
3			6

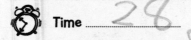

Solve the clues to complete this crossword puzzle.

Across

1. Erasable writing tool (6)
4. Once more (5)
6. Someone staying in a hotel (5)
8. Opposite of wide (6)

Down

1. Farmyard animal (3)
2. Small boat with a paddle (5)
3. Opposite of dark (5)
4. Nut from an oak tree (5)
5. Strong, aggressive feeling (5)
7. Female pig (3)

BRAIN GAME 70

Try and solve this 'Sudoku XV' puzzle. It's similar to a normal sudoku but with an added challenge to tickle your brain.

The Rules

- You must place the numbers 1 to 6 once each into every row, column and marked three-by-two area.

- There are 'x' and 'v' clues between some touching grid squares, which mean that the two numbers in those squares add up to either 10 or 5.

- If you see an 'x' then they add up to 10, and a 'v' means they must add up to 5. If you know Roman numerals this is easy to remember, because 'X' is the Roman numeral for 10, and 'V' is the Roman numeral for 5.

- All possible 'x' and 'v' clues are given. This means that if there is no 'x' or 'v' between a pair of touching grid squares then you know that they do not add up to 10 or 5. You'll need to remember that to solve this type of sudoku.

Here's an example solved puzzle to help you understand:

The 'v' means that the numbers in the touching squares must add up to 5.
3 + 2 = 5

The 'x' means that the numbers in the touching squares must add up to 10.
6 + 4 = 10

2	5	3	6	1 ᵥ	4
1	6 ˣ	4	5	3 ᵥ	2
6	2	5	1 ᵥ	4	3
4	3	1	2	5	6
5	4	2 ᵥ	3	6	1
3	1	6 ˣ	4	2	5

TOP TIP: If you need help getting started you could work out what other number must go next to each of the 'v's and 'x's which have numbers next to them already.

BRAIN GAME 71

Can you place a letter into each of the empty bricks in this word pyramid? When complete, each row will spell out a word that solves its corresponding clue.

Starting from the top and working down, each row contains the same letters as the previous row plus one extra, although they may be in any order.

For example, if the first row contained 'ACE' then the second row might add an 'R' to spell out 'CARE', and the row below that might add a 'T' for 'TRACE'.

a.

b.

c.

The Clues

a. Crazy.

b. If you build a model then you can say 'I _ _ _ _ this'.

c. You might have one of these when you are asleep.

d. To think of someone with great respect.

e. To make a mistake when looking at some words.

f. Fantasy, part-human creatures who live in the sea.

g. In the middle of a river.

h. Someone who is the clever genius behind a plan.

a.

b.

c.

d.

e.

f.

g.

h.

To solve these Calcudoku puzzles, place 1 to 4 once each into every row and column. You must place these numbers so that each bold-lined set of grid squares equals the small clue number printed in it when you write the clue's mathematical sign between the numbers in that area.

Look at this example:

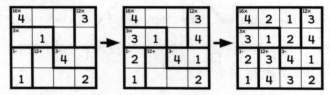

- For the four two-square areas, you need to find another number to go in each area that follows the rules above. For the '12x' area you can put in a '4', since 3 x 4 = 12. For the '1-' area you can write in a '2', since 2 - 1 = 1. You can solve the '3x' and '3-' areas in a similar way.

- Now you can complete the second and third rows, by remembering that you need to place 1, 2, 3 and 4 in every row and column. And once you've done that, you should be able to fill the rest in yourself using similar deductions.

a.

3+	11+	5+	2
	3	4	5+
6+	1	2	
6+ 4		4+	

b.

6x 3		8x	3x
9+	4		3
4	6x	1	
1-		1-	4

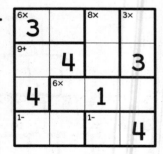

Use this word circle to try and solve the following clues. To make words, you must use the central letter plus two or more of the other letters. For example, you could spell the word 'MET'. You can start with any letter, but you can't use a letter more than once in a word.

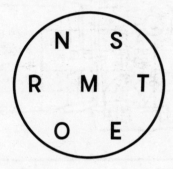

The Clues

a. The opposite of 'less'.

b. A poetic word for the first half of the day, before the afternoon.

c. This is a lecture that a priest might give in a church.

d. Someone who tutors you and guides your study.

e. A word for a male cat, and also a boy's name.

f. The green stalk of a plant is called this.

g. This word refers to a scary beast.

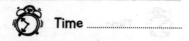

Boggle your brain with 'Windoku', a special kind of sudoku puzzle. Your challenge is to place the numbers 1 to 9 once each into every row, column, marked three-by-three area, as well as each of the four shaded three-by-three areas.

Psst! It's called 'Windoku' because the extra regions look a bit like windows.

	5	1				6	2	
2			1		9			4
9				6				8
	9			1			6	
		4	6		3	9		
	8			4			3	
7				2				5
8			7		6			3
	2	9				1	7	

By drawing along the existing lines, can you divide this shape up into four identical pieces, with no unused parts left over? If you imagine cutting the shape up into these four pieces, then each piece would have to be exactly the same once you rotated them all to point the same way. You can't turn any pieces over.

Have a look at this example. Can you see how you would have four identical shapes if you cut them out along the thick lines and made them all point the same way?

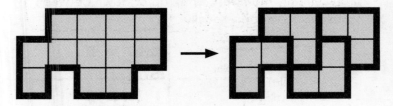

TOP TIP: Start by working out how big each piece must be. Because all the pieces must be the same size, you can count the number of grid squares and divide by four to calculate this.

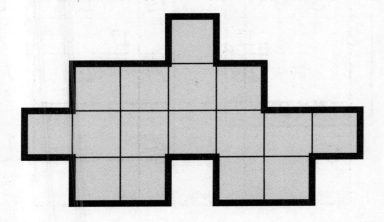

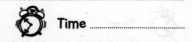
Can you fill in the empty squares so that the small grid
(Puzzle a) contains every number from 1 to 16 once each,
and the large grid **(Puzzle b)** contains every number from
1 to 25 once each?

The Rules

- You must be able to start at '1' and then move to
  '2', '3', '4' and so on by moving only to touching grid
  squares.

- You can only move left, right, up or down between
  squares, but not diagonally.

This example solution
should help make the
rules clear:

15	14	9	8
16	13	10	7
1	12	11	6
2	3	4	5

a.

	8	9	
2			11
3			16
	5	14	

b.

19		13		11
	17		9	
21		15		7
	23		5	
25		3		1

Using just your imagination, see if you can work out what computer keyboard symbol you would be able to form if you were to cut out and rearrange the positions of these six tiles. There's no need to rotate any of the pieces – just imagine sliding them to new positions.

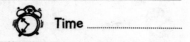
Solve these Futoshiki puzzles by placing the numbers
1 to 4 once each into every row and column.

You must obey the 'greater than' signs. These are arrows
which always point from the bigger number to the smaller
number of a pair. For example, you could have '2 > 1' since
2 is greater than 1, but '1 > 2' would be wrong because 1
is not greater in value than 2.

Here's a solved
puzzle to help you
understand:

	2	3
2 ◄		1
3	1	2

→

1	2	3
2 ◄	3	1
3	1	2

a.

		3	
		4	
	4		
	3		

b.

	>		2
		> 2	
		1	
		1	

These excitable dogs need to be kept under control.
Using only two straight lines, divide the park up into four
areas, with each area containing one tree, one dog and
one ball. The lines must start at one edge of the park and
cross all the way to another edge of the park. The lines will
need to cross each other in order to divide the park into
four areas. The lines must stay within the borders of the
main shape.

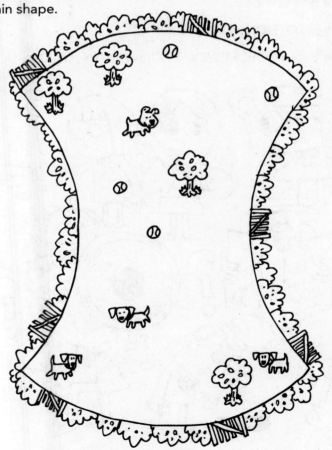

BRAIN GAME 80

Switch your brain to detective mode and see if you can reveal a hidden message in these codes. Use the clues on the opposite page to help you crack each line.

Code 1. TFDSFUUFYUGPMMPXT

Code 2. LTOHOEKBURNIDDEGRE

Code 3. FRHHDECD

Code 4. OTEIDNOE

Code 5. ASTIOEDERWEVAEEXIOALNMPYTUNKIAMUOE

The Clues

CODE 1: Replace each letter with the letter before it in the alphabet, so for example C becomes B. Insert two spaces to make three words.

CODE 2: Copy alternating letters on to two new lines, and then work out where to insert a space into each line to create four words.

CODES 3 AND 4: Take one letter from code 3, then one letter from code 4, then one letter from code 3, and so on until you have all the letters in a single row. Then work out where to insert three spaces to make four words.

CODE 5: Cross out every vowel except for every third vowel. You must also cross out every other consonant (first, third, fifth, etc), starting by crossing out the first consonant you come across. Insert three spaces into the remaining letters to make four words.

What is the final secret message?

....

....

....

....

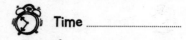
Solve this sudoku puzzle by placing the numbers 1 to 9 once each into every row, column and marked three-by-three area.

6	2						7	8
5	9		6		2		1	4
			9		8			
	7	1		9		8	4	
			8		4			
	6	4		2		5	3	
			3		9			
3	8		2		6		5	1
1	4						9	3

Can you find the 10 differences between these two very similar pictures?

BRAIN GAME 83

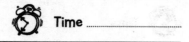

Time ....

Can you solve this crossword puzzle where all of the clues
are written inside the grid? The arrows show which grid
squares their solutions go in, and all words are written left
to right or top to bottom no matter which way the arrow
points. The first one has been done for you.

The taste of a food		What scissors do ►			
►					
Polite request word		Religious convent resident ►			
			Soft drink container		One after nine
			Used to row a boat		Family pet?
A climbing plant, often grows on buildings		Opposite of young ►			
►P	U	M	A	Common; everyday	
Type of big cat found in America		Small carpet ►			

Are you ready for the mighty 'Sudoku X'? Your mission is to place the numbers 1 to 9 once each into every row, column, marked three-by-three area and each of the two shaded diagonal lines.

		4	2	6	1	9		
	1			9			5	
6								7
8			5	3	7			9
2	7		8		9		1	5
5			6	1	2			4
1								2
	2			8			3	
		7	1	2	3	5		

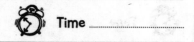
An anagram is a word that can be made by rearranging the letters of another word. For example, LEMON is an anagram of MELON.

Unscramble the anagrams below to fill in the missing words in these sentences. Each missing word is an anagram of the word written in capital letters in the same sentence.

a. Under the light of flickering _ _ _ _ _ , I admired the scene of tropical PALMS.

b. I've caught so many COLDS, my mother will _ _ _ _ _ me if I catch another one.

c. When my seeds _ _ _ _ _ _ _ _ , I was the PROUDEST I have ever been.

d. I walked by the LAKES and saw a lot of floodwater – I think one of them _ _ _ _ _ .

e. The _ _ _ _ _ _ moved so fast across the ice she was like a STREAK of light.

f. I didn't have time to sit on all of the royal _ _ _ _ _ _ _ because I had to SHORTEN my visit.

g. I went for a RAMBLE through the woods and came across some shiny _ _ _ _ _ _ rock.

Can you complete this crisscross puzzle by fitting all of the listed words into the grid, crossword-style?

TOP TIP: You could start by adding the nine-letter word in.

3 Letters	Mac	Rap	5 Letters
Air	Mud	Top	Cadet
Ape	Mum	Was	Hello
Boo	New		Toast
Eel	Nib	**4 Letters**	Whole
Hop	Own	Ache	
Lap	Pin	Mend	**9 Letters**
			Attempted

If you were to cut out these shape nets, which ones could you fold up to make a four-sided triangle-based pyramid, without any sides missing?

The folded-up pyramid shape would look like this:

a.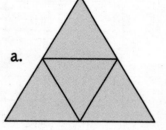

b.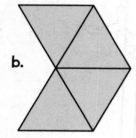

c.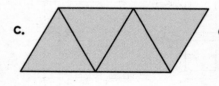

d.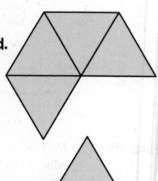

e.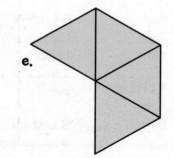

f.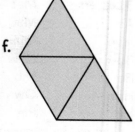

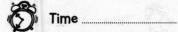 **Time** ....

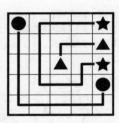

Can you draw lines to connect each pair of identical shapes together? The lines must not cross or touch each other, and only one line is allowed in each grid square. You can't use diagonal lines.

This example solution shows how it works:

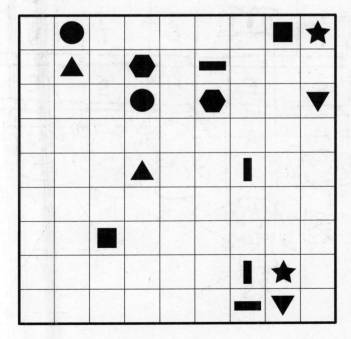

BRAIN GAME 89

Imagine sliding these columns of letters up and down to make different words through the horizontal window. One letter should remain visible through the window in each column. How many five-letter words can you make?

EASY TARGET: 5 words
MEDIUM TARGET: 10 words
HARD TARGET: 15 words

Time ....

Can your brain handle the 'Super Jigsaw Sudoku'? Solve the puzzle by placing a number from 1 to 6 in every square, but with no number appearing more than once in each row, column or bold-lined jigsaw-shaped area.

		2			3
2		6			1
					6
6					
1			3		4
3			6		

Time ....

Look at these dog faces.

a. How many dogs are there in total?

b. How many dogs are smiling?

c. How many unhappy dogs are there in the same row or column as a dog with its tongue out?

d. How many open eyes are there in total?

e. Without counting, how many closed eyes must there be in total?

f. Are there more sleeping dogs or more winking dogs?

How quickly can you crack these codes to find hidden words? To solve them you must delete one letter from each pair.

Here is an example. One letter is deleted from each pair to read 'TEST':

T~D~   ~A~E   S~K~   T~D~

a.   EF   AB   ST   XY

b.   DK   IS   DK   IS

c.   MN   EO   MN   EO   YN

d.   CR   LR   EI   TV   AE   RM

BRAIN GAME 93

Can you conquer these kakuro puzzles by writing a number from 1 to 9 into each of the white squares?

The Rules

- Place the numbers so that each continuous horizontal or vertical run of white squares adds up to the clue number shown in the shaded square to the left or top of that run.

- If a clue number appears above the diagonal line it is the total of the run to its right. If it appears below the diagonal line, then it gives the total of the run directly below the clue.

- You can't repeat a number in any continuous run of white squares. For example, to solve the clue number '4', you would have to use '3' and '1', since '2' and '2' would mean repeating '2'.

Have a look at this solved puzzle to see how it works:

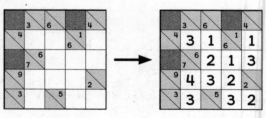

BRAIN GAME 94

Use your thinking powers to work out which grid squares contain hidden mines.

The Rules

- There can be a mine in any empty grid square, but not in any of the numbered squares.

- A number in a square tells you how many mines there are in touching squares, including diagonally.

Have a look at this example solution to see how it works:

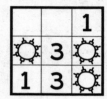

Now try these three puzzles:

a.

	2	0		
			3	2
2				
2		4		2
	1	1	1	

b.

1				4	2
	3				
3	4				
		3		2	
	2	1	1		
		0		2	

c.

	2		
1		2	
1	1		
		1	1

Psst! Puzzle C is a bit of a mindbender ... you'll need some clever thinking to solve it!

BRAIN GAME 95

 Time ....

Dig out your culinary skills and try to find all of the kitchen-themed words hidden in this wordsearch grid. They can be written in any direction, including diagonally, either forwards or backwards.

```
M E T E A S T R A I N E R S
O R B O T T L E O P E N E R
B U T T E R D I S H T L H O
E C E T N O R L S E A P S L
C T W T N O A A R C H C A L
R O R E C I O R S G A I M I
E A L N R R B N T N H T O N
M S S A C C E D O C D O T G
I T O I N H S P A T I P A P
T R E D C D E K E E C T T I
G A H T L N E H R E R I O N
G C I T E T H R A O L B P E
E K H R I G C T S L C E I N
A M I N E N A P G N I Y R F
```

BOTTLE OPENER
BREAD BIN
BUTTER DISH
CAKE TIN
CAN OPENER
CHEESEBOARD

COLANDER
CORKSCREW
EGG TIMER
FRYING PAN
KITCHEN SCALES
PEELER

POTATO MASHER
ROLLING PIN
TEA STRAINER
TOAST RACK

The four pieces needed to finish this jigsaw have been mixed up with some from a different puzzle. Can you find the four pieces needed to go in the gaps?

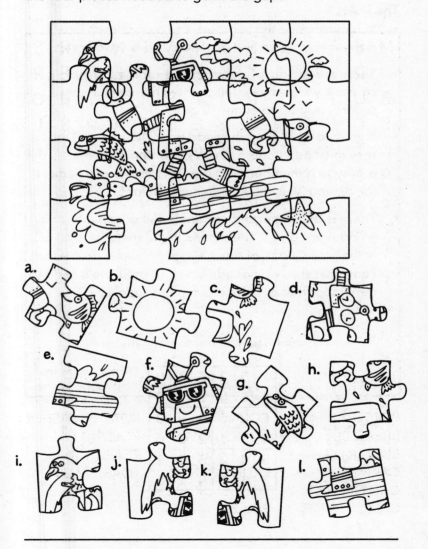

BRAIN GAME 97

Try and solve this 'Sudoku XV' puzzle. It's similar to a normal sudoku but with an added challenge to tickle your brain.

The Rules

- You must place the numbers 1 to 6 once each into every row, column and marked three-by-two area.

- There are 'x' and 'v' clues between some touching grid squares, which mean that the two numbers in those squares add up to either 10 or 5.

- If you see an 'x' then they add up to 10, and a 'v' means they must add up to 5. If you know Roman numerals this is easy to remember, because 'X' is the Roman numeral for 10, and 'V' is the Roman numeral for 5.

- There is one important extra rule. All possible 'x' and 'v' clues are given. This means that if there is no 'x' or 'v' between a pair of touching grid squares then you know that they do not add up to 10 or 5. You'll need to remember that to solve this type of sudoku.

Here's an example solved puzzle to help you understand:

The 'x' means that the numbers in the touching squares must add up to 10.
6 + 4 = 10

The 'v' means that the numbers in the touching squares must add up to 5.
3 + 2 = 5

2	5	3	6	1	4
1	6	4	5	3	2
6	2	5	1	4	3
4	3	1	2	5	6
5	4	2	3	6	1
3	1	6	4	2	5

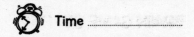
TOP TIP: If you need help getting started you could work out what other number must go next to each of the 'v's and 'x's which have numbers next to them already.

4ₓ	3		1ᵥ	6	
ᵥ		1ᵥ			ˣ
		ˣ	5	ᵥ	
		ˣ			
	2	6		5	4ᵥ

Can you rearrange the letters in order to spell out four numbers? All of the letters should be used once each.

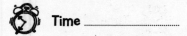
There's a vowel thief on the loose! Can you stop him by putting the vowels back to reveal what the original words were?

For example: XMPL ➡ **EXAMPLE**

a. GRDN

b. FMLY

c. SCHL

d. NTRTNMNT

e. QN

f. XT

g. Z

BRAIN GAME 100

Is your brain ready to shine? The aim of this game is to place lamps into some of the empty grid squares so that every remaining empty square is lit up by at least one lamp.

The Rules

- Lamps shine along grid squares in the same row or column right up to the first black square they come across. They don't shine diagonally.

- Some of the shaded squares contain numbers. These tell you exactly how many of the touching squares (up, down, left or right, but not diagonally) must contain lamps.

- A lamp isn't allowed to shine on any other lamp.

- You can place lamps on any empty square so long as the rules are followed.

Look at this before and after example:

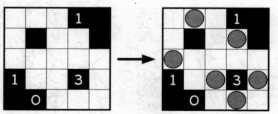

Notice how each of the numbered squares are touched by the same number of lamps.

If you imagine how each light shines you can see that this is the right solution. Every square is lit up, none of the lights shine on any other and the numbered clues have been followed.

TOP TIP: You can draw in the light shining from each lamp with a dashed line to make it clear.

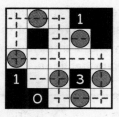

Now see if you can solve these puzzles.

a.

0			1		1
					1
3					
1		0			

b.

					2
	3				
					2
0					
				0	
0		2			

BRAIN GAME 101

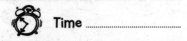

Are you ready for the mighty 'Sudoku X'? Your mission is to place the numbers 1 to 9 once each into every row, column, marked three-by-three area and each of the two shaded diagonal lines.

		5	3		7	4		
	8			9			7	
9		7				8		5
4				7				8
	7		2		8		4	
3				4				7
7		4				1		2
	2			5			6	
		6	9		2	7		

ALL THE ANSWERS

Brain Game 1

a.
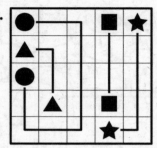

b.
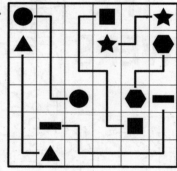

Brain Game 2

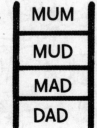

a.
CAT
COT
DOT/COG
DOG

b.
MUM
MUD
MAD
DAD

c.
THE
TIE
TIN
WIN

Brain Game 3

The correct jigsaw pieces are **b**, **c** and **d**.

Brain Game 4

a. There are 8 cubes on the bottom level (one of which is completely hidden) and 1 on the top level, making a total of 9 cubes.

b. There are 9 cubes on the bottom level (including one that is completely hidden – it must be there or else there'd be nothing holding up the cube above), plus 2 on the top level, making a total of 11 cubes.

Brain Game 5

Possible words are:

BEG	BUT	HIT	PIG
BET	DIG	HUG	PIT
BIG	DIM	HUT	PUG
BIT	DUG	HUM	PUT
BUG	HEM	PEG	
BUM	HIM	PET	

Brain Game 6

a.

b.

c.

Brain Game 7

Code 1. BEEN SEEN!

Code 2. MADE CODE BOOK?

Brain Game 8

a. To get the exact amount you would need 7 coins: 10, 10, 10, 10, 5, 2 and 1.

b. Three coins. You could use four coins for the exact amount (10, 10, 5 and 2), but normally when you buy something you don't have to give the exact change, so you could just use three 10 star coins which would add up to 30 stars – that's more than enough.

c. This isn't as complex as it sounds. To be able to make 33 stars exactly you need 5 coins: 10 + 10 + 10 + 2 + 1. It turns out you can also make 22 stars using those same coins (10 + 10 + 2), so you only need 5 different coins to be able to make either total.

d. Your change would be 37 stars, which would need a minimum of 5 coins: 10, 10, 10, 5 and 2.

Brain Game 9

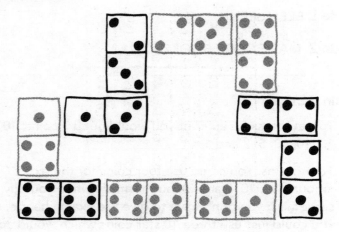

Brain Game 10

Brain Game 11

6	4	2	1	3	5
3	5	1	6	4	2
1	6	5	4	2	3
2	3	4	5	1	6
4	2	6	3	5	1
5	1	3	2	6	4

Brain Game 12

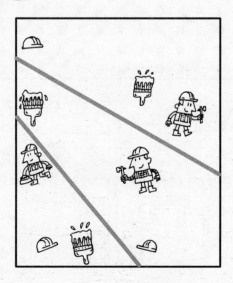

ALL THE ANSWERS

Brain Game 13

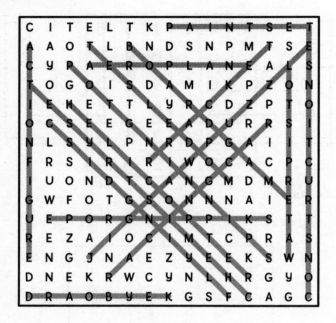

Brain Game 14

a. 30 bugs

b. There are more white bugs than black bugs (17 white and 13 black bugs)

c. 12 bugs

d. 11 bugs

e. 8 bugs

Brain Game 15

a.

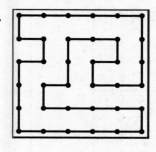

b.

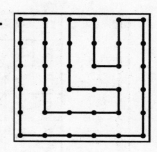

Brain Game 16

ALL THE ANSWERS

Brain Game 17

1	3	4	5	2	6
6	4	2	3	1	5
5	2	6	1	3	4
2	6	3	4	5	1
4	5	1	2	6	3
3	1	5	6	4	2

Brain Game 18

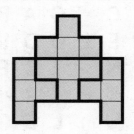

Brain Game 19

a. ACT

b. WASP

c. STRAY

d. CLAPS

e. POODLE

f. DANCER

Brain Game 20

a. 9 (2 is added at each step)

b. 32 (the value is doubled at each step)

c. 14 (3 is added at each step)

d. 1 (the value is divided by 3 at each step)

e. 14 (the value added increases at each step, so we have +1, +2, +3, +4)

Brain Game 21

a.

3	2	1
1	3 > 2
2	1	3

b.

3	4	2	1
2 > 1	3	4
1	2	4 > 3
4 > 3	1 < 2

ALL THE ANSWERS

Brain Game 22

Words that can be found include:

BALL	BEST	CAST	COTS
BASS	BETS	CATS	DELL
BATS	BOLT	CELL	DOLL
BELL	BOSS	COLT	DOLT
BELT	CALL	COST	DOTS

Brain Game 23

1	4	6	2	3	5
3	5	2	4	6	1
6	2	1	3	5	4
5	3	4	1	2	6
2	1	5	6	4	3
4	6	3	5	1	2

Brain Game 24

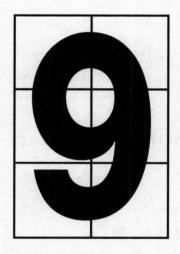

Brain Game 25

The hidden words are:
BADMINTON, SQUASH and TENNIS.

Brain Game 26

F	L	E	A		S		
E			T	A	U	T		H
D	U	S	T		M	U	T	E
			I			B		R
C	H	O	C	O	L	A	T	E
H		P			A			
E	V	E	N		B	Y	T	E
F		N	A	M	E			N
		P		L	O	U	D	

Brain Game 27

a.

10+ 3	3+ 1	2
1	2	3
5+ 2	3	1

b.

4+ 2	1	6+ 3
1	18× 3	2
3	2	1

c.

11+ 3	2× 2	1
2	1	3
2- 1	3	2

Brain Game 28

The pairs of monsters are:
a and **f**, **b** and **h**, **c** and **d**, and **e** and **g**.

Brain Game 29

a. RED

b. DEAR

c. AIR

d. DRAIN

e. READING

f. RING

g. RAIN

h. GARDEN

i. DARING

j. GRAIN

Brain Game 30

a.

7
2
5
10
6
3

b.

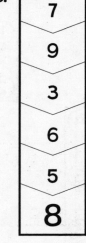

7
9
3
6
5
8

c.

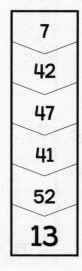

7
42
47
41
52
13

Brain Game 31

a. ATE

d. LATER

b. HAG

e. LATHER

c. LATE

The word using every letter is LAUGHTER.

Brain Game 32

a.

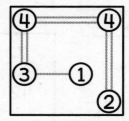

b.

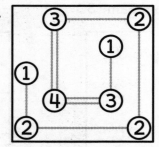

c.

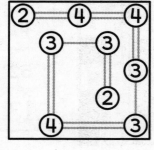

Brain Game 33

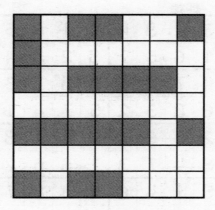

Brain Game 34

ALL THE ANSWERS

Brain Game 35

3	2	8	4	7	1	6	5
1	6	5	7	8	2	3	4
4	7	1	5	6	8	2	3
6	8	3	2	5	7	4	1
2	5	6	1	3	4	7	8
8	4	7	3	1	6	5	2
5	1	4	6	2	3	8	7
7	3	2	8	4	5	1	6

Brain Game 36

a. Calendar months: January, February, March, April, May, June, July, August, September, October, November and December

b. Colours of the rainbow: Red, Orange, Yellow, Green, Blue, Indigo and Violet

c. The numbers in order: One, Two, Three, Four, Five, Six, Seven, Eight, Nine and Ten

d. Race positions in order (these are called 'ordinal numbers'): First, Second, Third, Fourth, Fifth, Sixth, Seventh, Eighth, Nine and Tenth

Brain Game 37

a.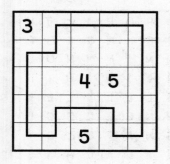

b.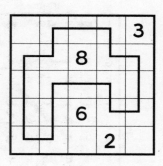

Brain Game 38

4	1	2	6	3	5
3	6	5	4	1	2
2	5	6	1	4	3
1	4	3	5	2	6
6	2	4	3	5	1
5	3	1	2	6	4

ALL THE ANSWERS

Brain Game 39

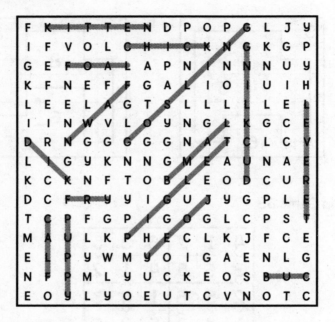

DID YOU KNOW?
A fry is a baby fish, and a leveret is a baby hare.

Brain Game 40

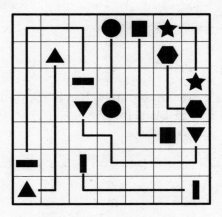

Brain Game 41

a. PLENTY (or **A**PLENTY is also a word)

b. M**A**RK

c. DR**EA**MING

d. KITCH**E**N

e. **AE**ROPLANE (you can also make **AI**RPL**A**NE, and the word **RE**PLAN)

f. BANANA (you can also make **B**UNION and **B**ONNIE)

g. TELE**V**ISION

h. **AA**RDVARK

ALL THE ANSWERS

Brain Game 42

a. 12 flowers

b. 66 leaves

c. 5 flowers

d. There are more white petals than black petals (68 white and 55 black petals)

e. 4 flowers

Brain Game 43

a. ACE

b. COOL

c. MAZE

d. BRAIN

Brain Game 44

2	7	3	6	4	5	1	8
5	8	1	4	7	6	2	3
6	1	8	3	2	7	4	5
7	5	4	2	8	3	6	1
3	6	7	1	5	2	8	4
4	2	5	8	3	1	7	6
1	4	2	5	6	8	3	7
8	3	6	7	1	4	5	2

Brain Game 45

The pairs of flowers are:
a and g, b and j, c and e, d and i, and f and h.

Brain Game 46

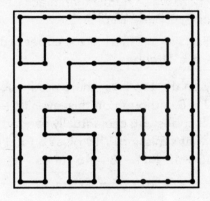

ALL THE ANSWERS

Brain Game 47

If you count each of the 4 layers of cubes from the bottom upwards, you should have worked out:

- 3 x 5 = 15 cubes on the bottom layer

- On the layer above it 3 cubes have been removed, so you have 15 − 3 = 12 cubes

- On the third layer up there are 4 cubes removed, so that's 15 − 4 = 11 cubes

- And finally on the top layer there are 7 cubes removed, and 15 − 7 = 8, although on this level it's easier to count the 8 cubes you can actually see rather than work out what's missing. This gives a total number of cubes of 15 + 12 + 11 + 8 = 46 cubes.

Brain Game 48

6	1 ‹ 2	4	3 ‹ 5
5	3	4 ‹ 6	2 › 1
2	5	3	1 ‹ 4 ‹ 6
1	4	6 › 3	5	2
4	2	1	5	6	3
3	6	5	2	1	4

Brain Game 49

a. SIS

d. MOP

b. POSE

e. ROSE

c. PROM

Extra Challenge: The word using every letter is PROMISES.

Brain Game 50

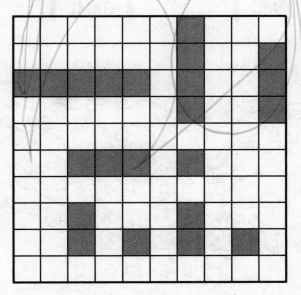

ALL THE ANSWERS

Brain Game 51

a.

HARD
HARE
HIRE
TIRE
TIME

b.

LONG
LONE
LANE
LAME
GAME

Brain Game 52

Brain Game 53

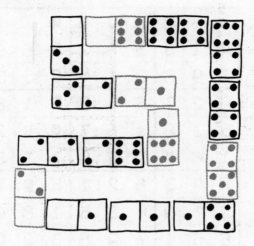

Brain Game 54

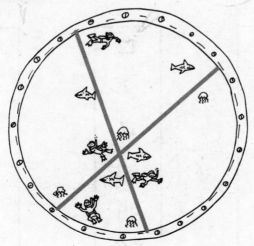

Brain Game 55

3	8	2	9	5	6	4	7	1
4	1	5	3	7	2	8	6	9
7	9	6	8	1	4	2	5	3
9	2	7	5	4	3	6	1	8
5	3	8	1	6	7	9	4	2
1	6	4	2	8	9	7	3	5
8	4	3	6	2	1	5	9	7
2	7	9	4	3	5	1	8	6
6	5	1	7	9	8	3	2	4

Brain Game 56

a.

16
4
24
5
17
7

b.

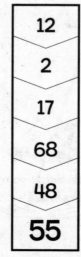

12
2
17
68
48
55

c.

20
33
28
45
32
64

Brain Game 57

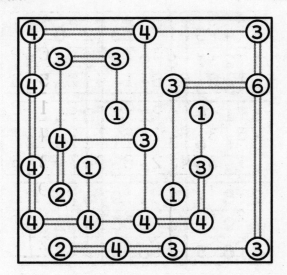

Brain Game 58

Words that can be made include:

BAN	BOT	COT	HAT
BAR	CAN	DAN	HEN
BAT	CAR	DEN	HER
BEN	CAT	DON	HOT
BET	CON	DOT	

DID YOU KNOW? 'Ben' is a Scottish mountain, a 'bot' is a type of computer programme, and 'dan' is a rating in a martial art such as karate.

ALL THE ANSWERS

Brain Game 59

6	4	9	1	5	3	2	8	7
1	2	7	8	9	6	5	4	3
8	5	3	4	7	2	1	9	6
5	1	6	9	2	7	8	3	4
9	7	8	3	4	1	6	5	2
4	3	2	5	6	8	7	1	9
2	8	4	7	1	9	3	6	5
7	9	1	6	3	5	4	2	8
3	6	5	2	8	4	9	7	1

Brain Game 60

a.

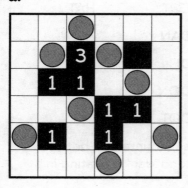

b.

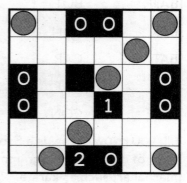

Brain Game 61

a.

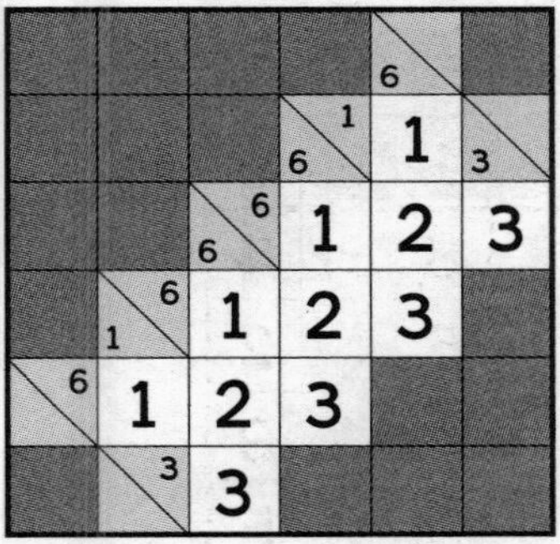

b.

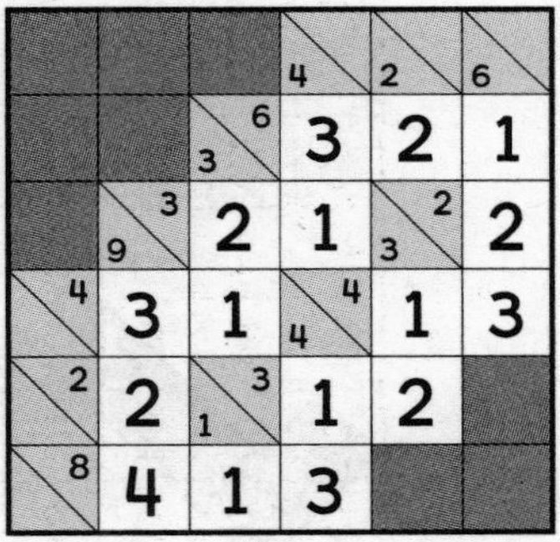

Brain Game 62

a. Top

b. Port

c. Sport

d. Poster

e. Protest

f. Protects

g. Spectator

ALL THE ANSWERS

Brain Game 63

The shapes that make boxes are **b**, **c** and **e**.

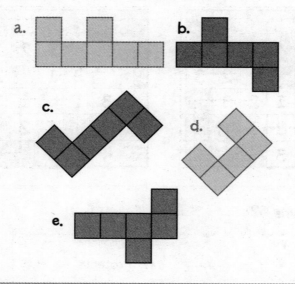

Brain Game 64

Brain Game 65

a.

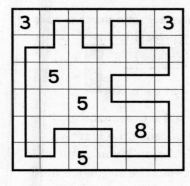

b.

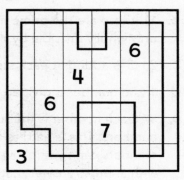

Brain Game 66

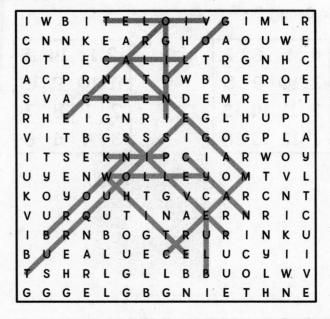

ALL THE ANSWERS

Brain Game 67

a. 7 (3 is subtracted at each step)

b. 11 (these are the prime numbers. Prime numbers are only wholly divisible by themselves and 1.)

c. 23 (5 is added at each step)

d. 1 (the number is divided by 4 at each step)

e. 37 (each number is the sum of the previous two numbers. This is hard to see because the first two numbers can't yet follow the rule, so if you came up with another answer that explains the sequence then that's perfectly valid, too!)

Brain Game 68

a.

4	5	6	7
3	10	9	8
2	11	14	15
1	12	13	16

b.

12	13	14	15
11	10	9	16
2	1	8	7
3	4	5	6

Brain Game 69

Brain Game 70

4	3	1	5	2	6
2	5	6	3	4ᵛ	1
6ˣ	4	3ᵛ	2	1	5
1	2	5	4ˣ	6	3
3	6ˣ	4ᵛ	1	5	2
5	1	2	6	3	4

ALL THE ANSWERS

Brain Game 71

a. Mad

b. Made

c. Dream

d. Admire

e. Misread

f. Mermaids

g. Midstream

h. Mastermind

Brain Game 72

a.

$^{3+}$1	$^{11+}$4	$^{5+}$3	2
2	3	4	$^{5+}$1
$^{6+}$3	1	2	4
$^{6+}$4	2	$^{4+}$1	3

b.

$^{6×}$3	2	$^{8×}$4	$^{3×}$1
$^{9+}$1	4	2	3
4	$^{6×}$3	1	2
$^{1-}$2	1	$^{1-}$3	4

Brain Game 73

a. More

b. Morn

c. Sermon

d. Mentor

e. Tom

f. Stem

g. Monster

Brain Game 74

3	5	1	8	7	4	6	2	9
2	6	8	1	3	9	7	5	4
9	4	7	5	6	2	3	1	8
5	9	3	2	1	8	4	6	7
1	7	4	6	5	3	9	8	2
6	8	2	9	4	7	5	3	1
7	3	6	4	2	1	8	9	5
8	1	5	7	9	6	2	4	3
4	2	9	3	8	5	1	7	6

Brain Game 75

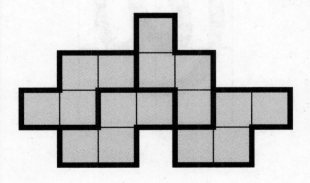

ALL THE ANSWERS

Brain Game 76

a.

1	8	9	10
2	7	12	11
3	6	13	16
4	5	14	15

b.

19	18	13	12	11
20	17	14	9	10
21	16	15	8	7
22	23	4	5	6
25	24	3	2	1

Brain Game 77

Brain Game 78

a.

4	2	3	1
3	1	4	2
1	4	2	3
2	3	1	4

b.

4 > 3	1	2
3	4 > 2	1
2	1	4	3
1	2	3 < 4

Brain Game 79

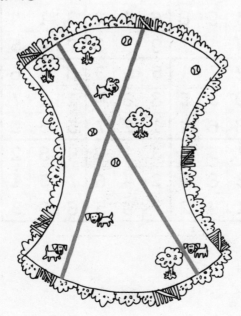

ALL THE ANSWERS

Brain Game 80

Code 1. SECRET TEXT FOLLOWS

Code 2. LOOK UNDER THE BRIDGE

Codes 3 and 4. FOR THE HIDDEN CODE

Code 5. TO REVEAL MY NAME

Brain Game 81

6	2	3	4	5	1	9	7	8
5	9	8	6	7	2	3	1	4
4	1	7	9	3	8	2	6	5
2	7	1	5	9	3	8	4	6
9	3	5	8	6	4	1	2	7
8	6	4	1	2	7	5	3	9
7	5	6	3	1	9	4	8	2
3	8	9	2	4	6	7	5	1
1	4	2	7	8	5	6	9	3

Brain Game 82

Brain Game 83

	F		C	U	T
P	L	E	A	S	E
	A		N	U	N
I	V	Y		A	
	O		O	L	D
P	U	M	A		O
	R		R	U	G

ALL THE ANSWERS

Brain Game 84

7	5	4	2	6	1	9	8	3
3	1	2	7	9	8	4	5	6
6	8	9	3	5	4	1	2	7
8	4	1	5	3	7	2	6	9
2	7	6	8	4	9	3	1	5
5	9	3	6	1	2	8	7	4
1	3	8	4	7	5	6	9	2
4	2	5	9	8	6	7	3	1
9	6	7	1	2	3	5	4	8

Brain Game 85

a. LAMPS

b. SCOLD

c. SPROUTED

d. LEAKS

e. SKATER

f. THRONES

g. MARBLE

Brain Game 86

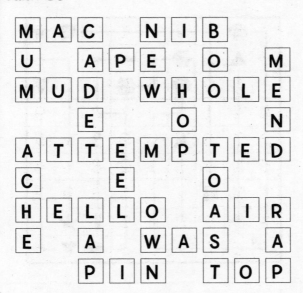

Brain Game 87

Only nets **a** and **c** fold up to make a four-sided pyramid. If that surprises you, try cutting them out and folding them up to see what shapes they make.

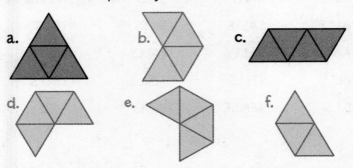

ALL THE ANSWERS

Brain Game 88

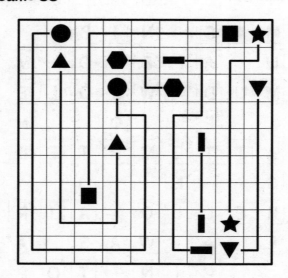

Brain Game 89

Words that can be found include:

MALLS	MINTS	SILLS	TENSE
MALTS	MINTY	SILLY	TENTS
MALTY	SALTS	SILTS	TILLS
MANLY	SALTY	TALLY	TILTS
MELTS	SELLS	TELLS	TINTS
MILLS	SENSE	TELLY	

Brain Game 90

4	1	2	5	6	3
2	3	6	4	5	1
5	4	1	2	3	6
6	2	3	1	4	5
1	6	5	3	2	4
3	5	4	6	1	2

Brain Game 91

a. 49 dogs

b. 33 dogs

c. 14 dogs

d. 69 open eyes

e. 29 closed eyes

f. There are more winking dogs than sleeping dogs (11 winking dogs and 9 sleeping dogs)

Brain Game 92

a. EASY

b. KIDS

c. MONEY

d. CLEVER

ALL THE ANSWERS

Brain Game 93

	3	12			3	4
4	1	3		4 / 20	1	3
9	2	7	11 / 11	8	2	1
	18	2	7	9	6	
	4	8 / 6	1	3	2	11
11	1	7	3	3	1	2
4	3	1		12	3	9

Brain Game 94

a.

☼	2	0		☼
☼			3	2
2	☼	☼	☼	
2		4	☼	2
☼	1	1	1	

b.

1		☼	☼	4	2
☼	3		☼	☼	☼
3	4	☼	☼		
☼	☼	3		2	
	2	1	1	☼	
		0		2	☼

c.

☼	2	☼	
1		2	
1	1		☼
☼		1	1

Brain Game 95

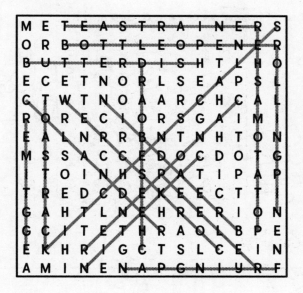

```
M E T E A S T R A I N E R S
O R B O T T L E O P E N E R
B U T T E R D I S H T L H O
E C E T N O R L S E A P S L
G T W T N O A A R C H C A L
R O R E C I O R S G A I M I
E A L N R R B N T N H T O N
M S S A C C E D O C D O T G
I T O I N H S P A T I P A P
T R E D C D E X E E C T T I
G A H T L N E H R E R I O N
G C I T E T H R A O L B P E
E K H R I G C T S L C E I N
A M I N E N A P G N I U R F
```

ALL THE ANSWERS

Brain Game 96

The correct jigsaw pieces are **c**, **d**, **e** and **k**.

Brain Game 97

4	3	5	1	6	2
6	1	2	4	3	5
3	5	1	2	4	6
2	6	4	5	1	3
5	4	3	6	2	1
1	2	6	3	5	4

You may have thought that the 5s and 2s in these squares could swap around, but this isn't the case. Remember the extra important rule, which says that all possible '**x**' and '**v**' clues are given. This means that if there is no '**x**' or '**v**' between a pair of touching grid squares then you know that they do not add up to 10 or 5.

If you swapped either of the 5s and 2s, the the 2s would each be next to a 3, but we know this cannot be correct because there are no '**v**' signs between these squares.

Brain Game 98

THREE   SIX

FIVE   SEVEN

ALL THE ANSWERS

Brain Game 99

a. GARDEN

b. FAMILY

c. SCHOOL

d. ENTERTAINMENT

e. QUEEN (although you can also make EQUINE, which means horse or horse-related, and QUOIN, which is an architectural term)

f. EXIT

g. ZOO, or OOZE if you prefer

Brain Game 100

a. **b.**

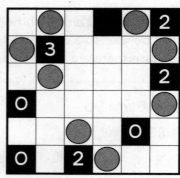

Brain Game 101

2	6	5	3	8	7	4	1	9
1	8	3	4	9	5	2	7	6
9	4	7	6	2	1	8	3	5
4	1	2	5	7	6	3	9	8
6	7	9	2	3	8	5	4	1
3	5	8	1	4	9	6	2	7
7	9	4	8	6	3	1	5	2
8	2	1	7	5	4	9	6	3
5	3	6	9	1	2	7	8	4

NOTES
AND
SCRIBBLES

NOTES AND SCRIBBLES

NOTES AND SCRIBBLES

NOTES AND SCRIBBLES

NOTES AND SCRIBBLES

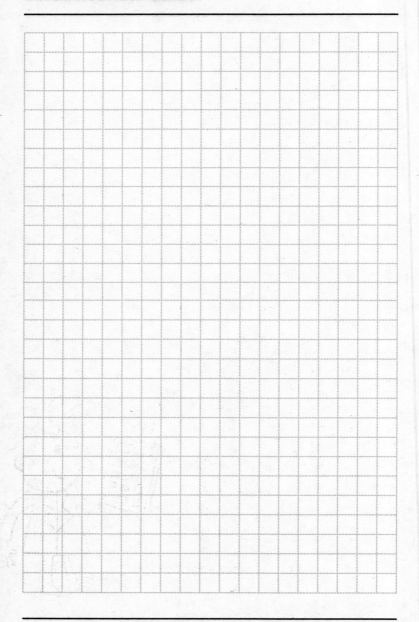

NOTES AND SCRIBBLES

NOTES AND SCRIBBLES

NOTES AND SCRIBBLES

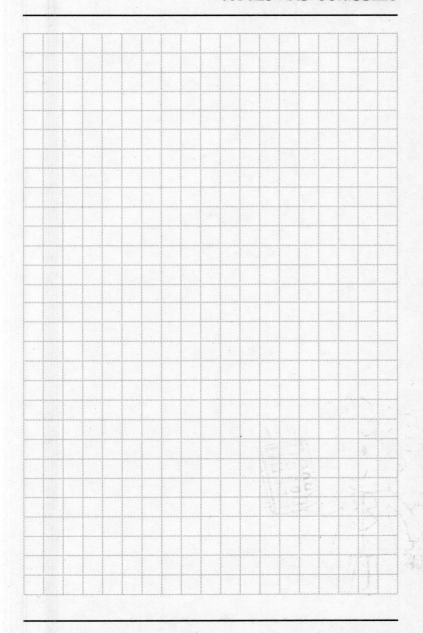

NOTES AND SCRIBBLES

ALSO AVAILABLE:

ISBN 9781780555638

ISBN 9781780555935

ISBN 9781780555621

ISBN 9781780554730

ISBN 9781780555409

ISBN 9781780554723

ISBN 9781780553146

ISBN 9781780553078

ISBN 9781780553085